Adapted and published in the United States in 1987
by Silver Burdett Press, 250 James St., Morristown, New Jersey
in association with Belitha Press Ltd., London.

Library of Congress Cataloging-in-Publication Data

Storr, Catherine.
    A fast move.

    (Let's read together)
    Summary: While their parents go by moving van
to the new house, Peter and Alison travel by train
with Gran and Grandpa, who are very forgetful.
    [1. Grandparents—Fiction.   2. Moving, Household—
Fiction]   I. Goffe, Toni, ill.   II. Title.   III. Series.
PZ7.S8857Fs   1987   [E]   86-31377
ISBN 0-382-09425-5
ISBN 0-382-09430-1 (pbk.)

Printed in Spain by Grafos

LET'S READ
TOGETHER

Catherine Storr

A FAST MOVE

illustrated by Toni Goffe

Silver Burdett Press
Morristown, New Jersey

Peter and Alison are going by truck
with all the furniture for the new house.
Grandma and Grandpa
are taking the twins
by train to meet them.

"I want to draw.
Where are my crayons?" Sally asks.
"I've lost my Friend Pig," says Tom.
"You can't have," says Grandpa.
"You're as bad as your Dad was
when he was your age."
"Let me find my handbag," says Grandma.

"Where will we meet Mom?" Tom asks.
"At the station," says Grandma.
"She'll drive us all to your new home."
"My keys! Where did I put them?"
cries Grandpa.

The man has come around
for the tickets.

"I'm sure I had them in my
handbag," says Grandma.

"No, they were in my secret pocket,"
says Grandpa.
But they're not.

"Who will get to the new house first?
Mom and Dad, or us?" Tom asks.
Cars are racing by on that road.
Are Mom and Dad in one of those trucks?

"I'm hungry," says Grandpa.

"I've got a tasty picnic here…
somewhere," Grandma says,
searching around.

"I'll go and buy something
to drink," Grandpa says.
"Where's my handbag?" Grandma says.
"It's got all our money and keys in it."

At the station they look for Mom and Dad.
"Where's Sally?" Grandma cries.
"She was here just now!"
"You lose everything, don't you?"
Tom remarks.

"Hurry! We've got the truck outside.
You'll have to sit on the furniture.
It'll be cramped," says Dad.
"Oh Tom, where's your cap?"

Now they're all at the door of the new house.
"Give me the front door key," says Dad.
"You had it," says Mom.
"Friend Pig is going to be happy here,"
says Tom.
"And so am I!" says Sally.